BASHFUL
BOB
and
DOLEFUL
DORINDA

MARGARET ATWOOD

BASHFUL BOB

and

DOLEFUL DORINDA

Illustrated by DUŠAN PETRIČIĆ

BLOOMSBURY
CHILDREN'S
BOOKS

Published by Bloomsbury Publishing, New York, London, and Berlin
Distributed to the trade by Holtzbrinck Publishers

Library of Congress Cataloging-in-Publication Data
Atwood, Margaret Eleanor.
    Bashful Bob and Doleful Dorinda / Margaret Atwood ; illustrated by Dušan Petričić.
        p.   cm.
    Summary: In this story told mainly with words that begin with the letters "b" and "d,"
    Bashful Bob, abandoned and raised by dogs, meets Doleful Dorinda, who deals with dirty
    dishes, and the two become fast friends and eventually heroes.
    ISBN-10: 1-59990-004-1 • ISBN-13: 978-1-59990-004-9
        [1. Friendship–Fiction. 2. Humorous stories.] I. Dušan Petričić, ill. II. Title.
    PZ7.A895Bas 2006   [E]–dc22   2006040111

First U.S. Edition 2006
Printed in China by South China Printing Co.
10 9 8 7 6 5 4 3 2 1

Book design by Peter Maher

Bloomsbury Publishing, Children's Books, U.S.A.
175 Fifth Avenue
New York, NY 10010

For Rowan—M.A.

To Rastko, my grandson,
who happened to arrive
at the same time as this book—D.P.

When Bob was a baby, he was abandoned in a basket, beside a beauty parlor. His bubbleheaded mom, a brunette, had become a blonde in the beauty parlor, and was so blinded by her burnished brilliance that baby Bob was blotted from her brain. By and by, she became dismayed, and bought an advertisement—"Baby in basket. Does not have a bat-shaped birthmark"—but it drew a blank.

Bob boo-hooed until he was blue from bonnet to bottom, but nobody came.

Luckily, beside the beauty parlor there was a vacant block, bestrewn with bushes, buttercups, and benches. It was beloved by dogs, who would bounce balls and bury bones there. A boxer, a beagle, and a borzoi heard Bob's bawling.

"Is it a buppy?" said the boxer, who talked through his nose.

"No, it's a biped," replied the beagle. "It must be a bird!"

"Not a bird, a baby! What bad behavior to abandon it!" barked the borzoi. "We must be benevolent!"

The boxer, the beagle, and the borzoi bounded into boutiques and burgled bundle buggies. They brought baby Bob bottles, booties, and blankets. When Bob became bigger, they brought bananas, blueberries, baked beans, beets, and broccoli. The broccoli made Bob burp.

The dogs were Bob's best buddies. They besieged bargain basements and brought Bob balloons, basketballs, blue jeans, and boxes of building blocks. They also brought bundles of buttered bread, barrelfuls of bran flakes, and bunches and bunches of blackberries. Bombarded with abundant edible boodle, Bob became even bigger. Soon he was no longer a baby, but a boy.

But Bob was bashful. He did not believe he was a boy and barked when bothered. He was bewildered by blithering barbers, blathering butchers, bun-bearing bakers, and belligerent bus drivers, and he would bound behind bushes or burrow under benches when they blundered by. He would bite busy businessmen in their briefcases.

"Bob is a boy," said the borzoi. "He does not belong with dogs."

"It is not broper," said the boxer.

"What will become of him?" said the beagle.

Bob's dog buddies were bemused.

On a block beside Bob lived Doleful Dorinda. Dorinda's dad and darling mother had disappeared in a dreadful disaster when she was still in diapers, and she had been dumped on distant relatives.

Dorinda was adorable, with dozens of dimples and a disarming charm. But although the distant relatives were dripping with diamonds and had a desirable address, they behaved despicably. They dispensed not a dollar on Dorinda; they didn't dole out a dime.

"Dorinda is a dope," they declared. "She is a dimwit. She is a drag. She is a dumb downer. Doleful Dorinda!"

They dressed Dorinda in dust rags and dingy dungarees. They made her doze on a dank and dubious duvet in a derelict dumpster, beside a deep drain full of deadly diseases, such as diphtheria.

She had to drudge from dawn to dusk, dabbing with a dust rag and dealing with dirty dishes in a disreputable dive, where dirty-deed-doers drank daiquiris. She had nothing to devour but defunct underdone duck; dangerously deep-fried day-old hot dogs; stale, dated doughnuts; and deplorable dairy products, deficient in vitamin D, and also disgusting. It was dire.

Dorinda became depressed. "Drat these darned dirty dishes," she declaimed. "I detest my distant relatives! I desire to be dealt with decently! I do not deserve such a dismal deal!"

One dark, drizzly December day, Dorinda departed. She packed some doughnuts and deplorable dairy products and several extra dust rags into a discarded duffel bag. "I defy doubt!" she declared. "Destiny, however distressing, will not defeat me! I disdain despair!"

Drenched by a downpour, dragging her duffel bag, and dreadfully bedraggled, Doleful Dorinda was trudging doggedly across Bashful Bob's

vacant block, when she heard a bark. Two bright but blinking eyes were beaming from behind a bush. Dorinda bent back a branch. It was not a dog but a bashful boy! "I am no desperado," said Dorinda. "May I share your domicile?" This was daring, as a barking boy might bite, but Dorinda was so damp she did not give a dastardly darn.

"*Bow wow*," barked Bob.

Dorinda decided to dedicate herself to teaching Bob to talk. The boxer, the beagle, and the borzoi were delighted! They burst into a bookstore and brought Dorinda and Bob a dictionary. Day by day, Dorinda and Bob delved into it. Though sometimes discouraged, Bob soon went from bite-sized words like "did" and "dot" and "bat" and "but" to difficult ones like "dirigible" and "ballistic."

"Bob is making brogress!" barked the boxer.

Bob beamed.

One day, a bewildered buffalo bounded over a barrier at a nearby botanical garden. It had been placed there by a befuddled and bungling bureaucrat, who had botched its diploma and declared it to be a big begonia.

"Beware! Beware! A dangerous beast!" bleated all the barbers, bakers, butchers, and bus drivers for blocks around, as they blundered in every direction.

The buffalo raised billows of dust. It dismembered daisies; it demolished daffodils and daycare centers. Horns beeped and blared. Businessmen blustered. Babies blubbered.

"Bob! Bob! We must do something!" beseeched Dorinda.

"Buffaloes bother me," said Bob. "They butt you in the behind. Besides, all those barbers, bakers, butchers, and bus drivers would behold me. That would make me bashful. I'd rather be in the burrow under the bench."

"No time for bashfulness," said Dorinda. "Duty beckons!"

Dorinda daringly distracted the buffalo by brandishing her dust rags and dancing like a dervish. Bob too behaved bravely. He deployed his dog buddies around the bewildered buffalo, and they all barked beautifully.

"Do not distrust us! We will not betray you!" barked the boxer, the beagle, and the borzoi. "You are not a big begonia, you are a buffalo! It was all a bureaucratic blunder!"

The buffalo, being bilingual, understood their barking and became benign. After devouring a bucketful of barley and a barrel of stale, dated doughnuts, it departed in a boxcar for Alberta, where it belonged.

"You are no longer Bashful Bob," declared Dorinda. "You are Brave Bob!"

"And you are no longer Doleful Dorinda. You are Daring Dorinda," said Bob.

"We will get our bictures in the bapers," said the boxer.

And they did.

Then Dorinda's dad and darling mother, who had been
digging their way out of the debris of the dreadful disaster
for dozens and dozens of days, recognized their
dear daughter Dorinda from her dimples.

Dorinda's distant relatives were dismayed
by the disclosure of their abysmal behavior, and
departed in disgrace.

And Bob's bubbleheaded mom, who was now a brunette again and had been deploring her distracted behavior at the beauty parlor, spotted Bob's biography in the paper. "He was abandoned in a basket! And he does not have a bat-shaped birthmark! He must be my baby, Bob!" she blurted, and she begged Bob's forgiveness. In addition, Bob's dad was gratified, as he had been distinctly disturbed by Bob's abrupt and baffling disappearance.

Together, all four parents bought a bungalow with abundant bedrooms, a dining room in which dishes of delicacies could be devoured, and a bounteous backyard, big enough for basketball and burying bones, with bunches of bushes behind which Bob could bound when feeling bothered, as he still did sometimes.

And so Brave Bob and Daring Dorinda and their parents—not to mention Bob's dog buddies, the boxer, the beagle, and the borzoi—dwelt in the bungalow in blinding bliss, delirious with delicious delight.